Happy Jack Meets the Archbishop
and Other Stories

Richard Adams

Amazon Kindle

Cover illustration includes manipulated image of Archbishop by Viktor Kolbus - **1743996143** from Shutterstock under license.

©Richard Adams 2024

In 2023 Richard Adams joined a
Writers Group which meets in the library
in the village of Ruddington,
Nottinghamshire.
Each fortnight the members submit
a story to the whole group by email.

On a Friday afternoon,
they comment on the submissions with a view
to improving their skills.
The stories are a random collection,
having been
based on a "prompt" (see Contents list)
provided by one of the members.

Richard Adams has been agreeably
surprised by the versatility that this approach
engenders and the variety of topics he has
found himself inspired to write about. He
hopes that his readers will be similarly
surprised and delighted.

Happy Jack Meets the Archbishop
and other stories

<u>Contents</u>

Happy Jack Meets the Archbishop
(prompt "Happy Jack")
1

Happy Jack TWO
(prompt "Confession")
8

Happy Jack THREE
(prompt "Criminals")
15

The Red Barn
(prompt "Summer Adventure")
23

Mouse Meeting
(prompt "Animal")
30

Christmas Cottage
(prompt "Christmas Card scene")
36

Tonsorial Artist
"prompt "Where did he go?")
42

Mystery Man
(prompt "Mystery Man")
51

Not the Two Ronnies
(prompt "Put two people in a room")
60

Mrs Grace's Journal
(prompt "Found Book")
66

As I walked Out
(prompt "As I walked out")
75

Happy Jack Meets the Archbishop

The weekly satirical magazine *Privet Edge* was running a cartoon strip about Happy Jack. In reality, Happy Jack was Igor Appijjhaak the president of the Cascaran Republic, and had he known the extent to which he was being lampooned on a regular basis, there is no doubt he would have arranged for the editor of *Privet Edge* to be arrested or disappeared in one of the many ways he had at his disposal.

However, while the politicians and diplomats of the United Kingdom, laughed and admired the sharp wit being employed to ridicule a man who considered himself all powerful and invulnerable, the man himself was, for the moment, unaware of it.

President Igor Appijjhaak was in his office in the city of Muskrat in the Greater Republic of Cascara, seated at a spacious desk of rich mahogany inlaid with green leather, lit by brass lamps polished to perfection. He liked to surround himself with the trappings of power. He embraced opulence. Others would have called it ostentatious, but it pleased him. The walls of the office were hung with paintings and tapestries depicting medieval battles and portraits of the bemedalled generals and captains whose strategies had served to defeat their past enemies. The fact that the portrayals were figments of the artist's imagination, worried Igor Appijjhaak not a bit. They were reflections of the power he assumed as his presidential right and let no one dare forget it. If anyone thought that the Greater Republic of Cascara was so called because there was, somewhere, a smaller republic of Cascara, they were free to think it, but the Greater Republic of Cascara was simply greater than anyone else's republic of whatever name or nationality. This geographical sleight of hand was a conceit which amused the president greatly.

The office in which Igor Appijjhaak sat was housed in what appeared to be a medieval castle, but it was very much twentieth century, hiding within its granite façade and Disney-like towers, as much protective technology, and espionage devices as could be inconspicuously installed in its floors, walls, and ceilings. Cameras and video screens were deliberately allowed to be on view in chosen places, as a reminder that you were being watched and unlikely to get away with anything furtive or subversive. Even the two uniformed armed guards standing stiffly to attention outside Igor Appijjhaak's office felt intimidated. It was a relief to both, when one of them heard the president's voice in his earpiece announce, "Bring him in."

The visitor was Archbishop Elymas of the Cascaran Orthodox Church, a thin man whose leanness was hidden beneath his ornate, heavily embroidered cope and mitre. The mitre made him taller than either of the guards and made him an imposing presence. His real name was Ivan Petrovich. As the guards moved towards him, he rose from the seat in the anteroom where he had been waiting for almost an hour. He was unsure if he should regard this audience with Igor Appijjhaak an honour. He was surprised that it had been granted at all, and he followed the guards somewhat nervously as they opened the double oak doors of the President's office and showed him in. They indicated with their rifles that he should sit in a highbacked chair with tapestry upholstery positioned, facing the president, at what Igor Appijjhaak regarded as a safe and respectful distance. The two guards stood one on each side of him.

The archbishop risked offending protocol by speaking first. He eyed the guards pointedly and said, "I had hoped we might speak freely."

Igor Appijjhaak paused. From the very start, the priest had discomfited him; but then, he considered, the archbishop was a man of God, a man of peace, surely, not a potential assassin. Igor Appijjhaak decided he would show no fear and nodded to the guards that they should leave. They closed the doors behind them, and the president and his visitor were left together unattended, except for the watchful eyes of the hidden cameras. Ivan Petrovich was also aware that strictly speaking, they were not unattended. He was a priest, but he was not a fool. Somewhere in a distant room with a bank of high-definition monitors and stereo sound would be officers of the president, with headphones, listening to every word and watching for any suspicious move.

"Igor," Ivan began.

"You will address me as Mr. Appijjhaak, or Mr President," said Igor.

Ivan ignored the rebuke and asked, "Would you say you were a Christian?"

After a moment to recover himself, Igor said, "I believe so."

"Belief is neither faith nor commitment," said Ivan, gaining confidence. "But, setting that aside, as a Christian, I choose to address fellow Christians by their *Christian* names. Perhaps we could agree."

Igor mumbled something incoherent which Ivan took as agreement, and pressed on, "I sent you a letter."

Igor pulled a piece of paper across the desk and held it up, "I have it here," he said and read it aloud, "I have a deep concern for your soul. May we speak?"

"I am grateful that you invited me to come," said Ivan.

"It is unprecedented," replied Igor, "You are privileged."

In London, having been texted by an employee who had managed to infiltrate the news operations of Cascara, the editor of *Privet Edge* was trying to contain his astonishment at these *unprecedented* developments, and wondering what variations he could spin on Happy Jack and the Archbishop. In the graphics of the cartoon strip, the face of the President of Cascara would be *drawn* in more ways than one.

"You know that I only have to press a button beneath this desk and the guards will return and arrest you," said Igor. You would do well to remember who you are speaking to. Respect, Archbishop, respect."

Ivan stood up. The President looked up at him and felt compelled to stand up too, to offset the dwarfing effect of a tall archbishop in his stately regalia. He suddenly felt unaccountably small. Ivan removed his mitre, moved forward, and placed it on the desk. He removed his cope and walked back to the chair to drape the heavy circle of material over the seat of it. Now he was plain Ivan Petrovich, in a thin grey suit and badly knotted tie."

Two powerful men stood looking at each other. In the observation room, the officers were holding their breath and one of them moving a hand towards the alarm button.

Ivan readied himself for the speech which he had rehearsed over and over again in the presbytery. He knew that within the church he was a powerful man, but he chose to modify his power with understanding and compassion. He was shepherd to a flock. He would even include the man in front of him in that flock. "Igor," he said, "Here we both are. Two men. We both came out of our mother's wombs with nothing, and in different spheres have risen to positions of authority, but in one thing we are no different from each other. You, like me, and every other human soul will go to the lavatory, and you will sit on a cold seat with your trousers round your ankles and empty your bowels with noise and stench and have no one to wipe you clean but yourself." With that, Ivan slid the belt from his trousers and dropped them to the floor. He had purposely foregone the protection of underpants and stood proudly in front of the president who was too startled to respond.

In the observation room there were loud guffaws until they remembered it was an arrestable offence to laugh at the president. They were certainly not laughing at the archbishop who quickly pulled up his trousers and knocked at the double doors for the guards to release him. He hurried down the steps of the Government Offices to be greeted with cheers by the waiting crowds who had been listening on their mobile phones to every word conveyed by the small transmitter secreted in Ivan's mitre. A waiting car sped him swiftly to safety across the Cascaran border where a new appointment was prepared for him in the Cathedral City of Happysburg in the Republic of Meltz.

Igor Appijjhaak, President of the Greater Republic of Cascara, fell back with a thump into his chair and fumbled in a desk drawer for a glass tumbler and a bottle of vodka with which he attempted to revive his wilting ego. He stared at the archbishop's cope and mitre which his visitor had left behind. He had not been assassinated but it felt as though he had.

In London, the editor of the *Privet Edge* had his strapline for the next episode of Happy Jack.

"Jack-hammered by Archbishop's Regalia." It was euphemistic, but it was true, and Igor Appijjhaak would not quickly forget it.

Happy Jack TWO

When the two guards on duty outside President Igor Appijjhaak's office had stopped laughing and satisfied themselves that the Archbishop in plain clothes who had scurried past them was of no danger to the president or anyone else, after a nervous tap at the great oak doors and receiving no response, pushed one of them open to find the President still slumped in his chair, the bottle of vodka, half consumed.

They had orders not to speak to the president unless he spoke to them first, but Igor Appijjhaak was clearly in no fit state to issue orders or even bid them good day. Finally, one of the guards took the risk and said, "Mr President, can we be of assistance?"

Igor Appijjhaak did not answer. His face appeared to be fixed in a twisted grimace. They radioed for a doctor.

Dr Serge Oblomov came at once. He would not have delayed for a moment given that it was the president's health that appeared to be at stake. On his arrival he summoned an ambulance which took the president with blue lights flashing and sirens blaring to the Cascara State Hospital and to a private ward which accommodated only those of high rank and was therefore almost always empty.

"I would say it was some form of Catatonic shock," Dr Oblomov told the Consultant who greeted him, and the Consultant nodded agreement. "Paranoia," he added, "Do we know of anything which might have triggered this reaction?"

Enquiries were made, but no one seemed inclined to make fools of themselves, despite the digital recordings of what had taken place in the President's office, by suggesting that the attack had been triggered by an archbishop's flagrant exposure of his genital regalia, after a short, colourful, if somewhat crude, sermon on how the functions of one's bowels placed everyone on the same level. Surely, they argued, Igor Appijjhaak was immune to such a simple psychological admonition. Or was he more vulnerable than he appeared?

Nurses were called, who nervously but efficiently undressed the president and clothed him in a pale blue hospital gown and connected him to an I.V. drip designed to counteract the alcohol streaming through his veins and stimulate him back to consciousness.

Other than that, nobody seemed to know what to do, except to wait for the effects of the encounter with Archbishop Elymas to wear off. Routine blood tests revealed nothing to account for Igor's condition.

Meanwhile in the absence of orders from the president himself, and any obvious course of action, the head of the JCB (Justice and Criminality Bureau) Alexander Thikkskinn, stepped in and decided to pursue the audacious Archbishop. His getaway car had been tracked as far as Bendix, where the fugitives had stopped to refuel and use the toilets, but they fooled their pursuers by going back the way they had come for several miles with blazing undipped headlights which made them invisible to oncoming traffic and their pursuers in particular. Calculating with great speed and accuracy a notorious bend, they drove towards their pursuers who misjudged the bend completely, lost control of their Mercedes and hurtled blindly through a fence and across a ploughed field where they became embedded. The archbishop and his friends continued their journey unhindered, using a maze of secondary roads, while their pursuers reported frustratedly to headquarters and returned by train in muddy boots to relate their failure to Alexander Thikkskin. He resolved in due course to track down the archbishop in his new post and poison the communion wine. "We have ways of dealing with this sort of mischief," he muttered.

It was early the next day that the president opened his eyes and in a sad whimper was heard to say, "Moya mat. Are you there, moya mat?"

The single guard who had been assigned to him overnight, radioed to the consultant, "He is awake, and asking for his mother."

Mrs Appijjhaak had shrugged off the status of being a president's mother, refused the offer of a grand house in the city suburbs, and gone to live in a remote village on the outskirts of the Republic. It would be at least half a day before she could be contacted and brought to her son's bedside. She had never thought of her son as anything better than an arrogant teenager once he had turned thirteen, and she thought of him even now as a selfish, ignorant pig-headed fifty-four-year-old fool. She had taken no pride in his being elected president. She knew full well it would have been naked ambition at the expense of others that had taken him there. She bitterly resented travelling halfway across the Republic to see him in hospital. What could he possibly want from her that he could not have cajoled out of someone else with a fat bribe or the prospect of *disappearance*? But a son was a son. He was her flesh and blood after all. She knew about unconditional love, and she honoured that virtue in spite of everything.

In appearance she might have been mistaken for a peasant woman, dressed as she was in a floor length brown smock dress with a grey shawl over her shoulders and a headscarf tied under her chin. Divorced unhappily from her aimless husband for forty-six years, she was now seventy-three and walked with a slight stoop as she followed a nurse down the long, spotless corridor which led to her son's private room.

The nurse had propped the president up on a heap of pillows, the better to greet his mother, but he was not entirely alert. "Is that you, moya mat?" he said, his eyes seeing her shape but failing to focus. The nurse brought a chair to the bedside, and Mrs Appijjhaak sat down, but made no attempt to reach for her son's hand. He had been a stranger for too long and he was no longer a child.

"Well, Igor," she said, "And now what have you been up to?"

"I have sinned," said Igor, as though confessing to a priest, "I have done those things I ought not to have done, and I have not done those things that I ought to have done."

"And there is no health in us," added his mother, reciting the familiar liturgy, "You are ill, Igor, and nobody knows what is wrong with you."

The door opened quietly. The consultant slipped in to stand behind her and was listening. "It is a form of dementia," he said, "It is surprising how quickly it can sometimes develop. Not that that tells us very much, other than that he is confused and suffers from memory loss."

"He has always suffered from memory loss," Mrs Appijjhaak replied, "If he was evidently to blame for some misdemeanour when he was younger, he could never remember even being there."

"That's selective memory," said the consultant, "All children are prone to it."

"He was thirty-six," his mother said promptly, "A house mysteriously caught fire and three election candidates died in the flames. Igor said he was on holiday in Liarsburg, but I knew otherwise."

They had both forgotten that even though those who have dementia, paranoia or some variation of catatonic shock are often temporarily dumb, they are not necessarily deaf. Igor had been listening.

"It is true," he croaked, "I have paved my way to power by denying and destroying the potential of others. No one was good enough but me to rule the Republic. The inadequate and disagreeable had to be prevented."

"He means eliminated," said his mother. "Will he recover, do you think, and rule again?"

"Possibly," said the consultant, "Possibly not. Now if you will excuse me, I must administer some medication. You may prefer to leave."

Mrs Appijjhaak had no desire to stay and left the room. After a short interval the consultant joined her on a bench in the corridor. Briefly he had a vision of a young couple seated similarly on a moonlit night by the river. The vision was soon gone.

"Confession has brought him peace," he said to her.

A moment passed in which neither of them could find anything to say. Mrs Appijjhaak found herself looking sideways at the consultant and wondering why his presence slightly disturbed her. Then from her son's room there came a loud bang. They both rushed in to find Igor with his head on a blood-soaked pillow, most of his face in shattered fragments. A revolver slid from his hand to the floor with a clatter.

Mrs Appijjhaak looked at the consultant. "But how?" she said, "How did he have a gun?"

The consultant shook his head. "I fear that his condition will not permit him to remember," he said, and left the room, leaving a bereaved mother by her son's lifeless, blood-spattered body, wondering whether or not she should grieve.

She decided not, and after a moment of revelation, followed her ex-husband out of the hospital, grateful that for once in his life he had done something decisive.

Happy Jack THREE

"You must stay strong," said Yeva, to her husband Alexander, the Head of the Cascaran JCB (Justice and Criminality Bureau).

"I am always strong, my little Kurita," said Alexander Thikskinn, but he was strong only because in her company, she was his little chicken and he was her petukh, her rooster, no matter that she was still not pregnant and he feared he might be infertile. They tried not to mind.

"Then stay strong," Yeva repeated, "You are not to blame."

Alexander Thikskinn had always been able to convince himself that he was not to blame. The escape of the mischievous archbishop across the border after his frightful exhibition in front of President Igor Appijjaak was not his fault, but that of the men who had been sent to pursue and arrest him. It was they who had failed.

They had been summarily disappeared and would never reappear.

The dilatoriness of the guard at the Cascara State Hospital whose momentary incontinence had permitted an assassin to enter the President's sick room and blow his brains out; that was not his fault either. The guard had also become a victim of the Master of the Art of the Disappearing Trick.

"Yes, I am the Master. I learned the Art of making people disappear from the Grand Master Igor Appijjaak," Thikskinn reassured himself, as Yeva crawled onto his lap on the capacious sofa, barrenness proving all the greater incentive to sexual appetite. She began to unbutton his shirt and empty the remains of a bottle of champagne onto his chest. Alexander Thikskinn did not feel strong enough either to resist or respond to her advances.

Then he remembered that he ought to have initiated an investigation into the whereabouts of the assassin who had taken the president's life, but without direct orders to do so from the president himself who was clearly indisposed, he was uncertain what to do. Igor's death had given him a curious freedom which he found difficult to handle, although he had taken advantage of it on this particular evening.

Yeva and he were luxuriating in a private apartment which Igor Appijjhaak had installed in a secluded part of the government offices. Access was possible only by a Wi-Fi operated entrance to which only Igor had the codes, but on one occasion he had succumbed to temptation and shared them with Alexander. After all, where was the pleasure in possessing such opulence if you could not swank about it? There were no hidden cameras or microphones. The usual intrusive surveillance was deliberately absent. "Even the president should not always know what the president is up to," Igor had joked in a rare moment of humour.

Igor had oozed smugness as he ushered Alexander into a spacious high-ceilinged room from which there hung a glistening modern chandelier in the form of a kinetic mobile with shards and splinters of opaline glass dispersing the light. Plain white walls were hung with large abstract paintings in subtle monotones. There was a bar with gleaming optics and glassware, and a small but lavishly equipped kitchen which would have catered for a large family, though Igor confessed he had only once partaken of a light supper of scrambled egg and smoked salmon – with champagne, of course. The piece de resistance was a bathroom of green-veined marble with gold fittings. A white monogrammed bath robe hung on the back of the door.

If there was a bedroom, Alexander never discovered it. Quite suddenly, Igor had left Alexander with his mouth agape at the dazzle of the bathroom, and dashed across the room to the bar, behind which he disappeared for a moment, to rise up again clutching two small cellophane packets and tossing one of them across to him. "You should try these," said Igor, "I discovered them when I was in a gostinitsa in London. They say *a public house*. I have them imported specially."

Alexander could not translate the label on the packet. "What are they?" he asked.

"Scratchings of pork," Igor told him, "Delicious. No?"

Alexander broke open the packet and felt obliged to enthuse, but to himself he admitted he did not like the flavour, the greasiness, or the prospect of breaking his teeth on the hard bits.

However, Alexander confessed privately that his strength had come from this proud, extravagant, childish, ruthless but now inevitably *late* president, and without him he was nothing. As second in command he now had a state funeral to arrange and, when that was done, he would have to manage and manipulate the machinery of an election. The assassin would have to wait for a while.

The sofa on which the inebriated couple were sprawled was one of three. All were shades of white with large white cushions and appliqued throws. White wool rugs softened the space in front of each. Yeva wondered who did the cleaning.

Other furniture was minimal - a small white lacquered dining table and two matching chairs, small side tables, some against the walls between the paintings, and others at coffee table height spaced at random for books, flower containers - with artificial lilies, assorted plates, drinking vessels as required, and the occasional, semi abstract sculpted figure. Everything was white. It had saved Igor the tedium of choice. The interior designer had relished the simplicity, but charged an exorbitant fee nonetheless, which Igor had not disputed. It was not his money after all.

Yeva, apparently no longer of interest to Alexander who had begun to snore, had fallen to gazing around at the room and wondering just who had paid for it.

"Was the president rich?" she said aloud.

Alexander woke with a start, "What?"

"The president," Yeva said, "Was he rich? Where did he get his money? Who paid for all this?"

Alexander wondered how much he should divulge, and then remembered he no longer had Igor breathing down his neck. "My poor little Kurita," he said at last, "My poor innocent chicken."

"Innocent?"

"Every bill that Igor incurred was sent directly to the Finance Department and settled in full."

"And no one questioned it?"

"People who asked questions tended to disappear."

Yeva was suddenly gripped by a terrible revelation. "The people of the Republic of Cascara have paid for this?"

"In a manner of speaking." said Alexander, "Not to mention much, much more! How do you think we are able to live in a fine house and enjoy our comfortable lifestyle?"

Too much champagne had loosened his tongue, but he was also relishing the freedom of being able to admit the truth at last.

Yeva looked at her husband with wide and staring eyes. "The common people have paid the price. They have lived in fear, and ….." she paused, hardly able to absorb and express the dreadful realisation. "You are Head of the JCB. We have lived at the expense of the people you are supposed to protect."

"In truth," added Alexander Thikskinn, "I protected no one but the president."

"And yourself," Yeva said flatly.

Alexander drew his wife to him and kissed her gently on the forehead. "And because I love you, I protected you too, my little chicken."

"Then the two of us are criminals," said Yeva, "You should arrest us both." They laughed at that, and then thought it was really no laughing matter and stopped guiltily.

They fell asleep in each other's arms and Alexander had a dream in which he saw the crowds and heard the cheers that had greeted Archbishop Elymas on his departure from the office of President Igor Appijjhaak on the day of his catatonic seizure. He reflected that by the mischief of a solitary archbishop the course of history might be about to turn.

He awoke to the sound of the kinetic chandelier turning and tinkling above his head and the smell of cooking. Yeva was busy in the kitchen.

"Ah," she called to him, "You are awake. I am making breakfast." Set almost invisibly into the kitchen wall was a refrigerator, opened silently at the touch of a button. She had found eggs, bacon, and mushrooms, and was making an omelette.

For a moment, as she whisked the eggs in a glass bowl, she wondered how and by whom the stock was replenished, but no matter now, the fat in the pan on the bright black hob was hot.

As they sat together at the dining table, Alexander found himself wondering how many people had died eating mushrooms before they had learned which were poisonous and which were not. History was an omelette, he decided, cooked by trial and error and breaking eggs.

"There will be an election," he told Yeva, "Rigorous, honest, transparent, with candidates nominated from amongst those who have been disappeared into prisons and labour camps or early graves under Igor Appijjaak's presidency, those who had been unsatisfied with being told what they must think. For a while the enforced stability of the Republic of Cascara will wobble, but there are enough decent, honest people to steady it."

"You sound as though you are making a campaign speech, "Yeva said, "You know that after such a tight regime, people will be confused. They will not know who to trust. There will be pandemonium."

"You are not so innocent after all," Alexander replied, "But better pandemonium than revolution," and he mopped up the remains of his omelette with the last crust of the tastiest bread he had ever eaten.

"And somewhere in the midst of all this," asked Yeva, "Might we strive to have children?"

"Definitely," said Alexander, but not, Yeva detected, with total confidence. She stretched her hand across the table and laid it on his.

"Stay strong, my brave Rooster," she said," Stay strong."

The Red Barn

"Are you there?"

It's my mother, shouting from the kitchen. I am in the shed, making a balsa wood glider.

"You're always *somewhere*," she says, which I can't quarrel with. "Where's your sister?"

I can see Mum through the shed window. She leaves the kitchen through the back door of the house and crosses the square concrete slabs in four strides that bring her to the shed. She pulls open the door.

"Where's your sister?"

"How should I know?"

My fingers are all gluey and I wipe them down my trousers.

"Don't do that," she says, "It'll never come off. Where's Sally?"

My sister Sally is six. I am ten. It is the summer holidays and I'm supposed to keep an eye on her. I suddenly remember. "She went with Jenny Mynard."

"Went where?"

I am trying to remove the glue from my fingers by chewing at them. The taste is awful.

"How do you know that's not poisonous?" says Mum. "Get indoors and use a scrubbing brush."

In the kitchen with the tap running, I scrub at my fingers with a nail brush. "Use some Vim," says Mum, "Have you remembered?"

"What?"

"Where they went. Our Sally and Jenny Mynard."

"Oh, yeah. They said they were going on an adventure." I dry my hands on a towel and make my way back towards the shed.

"They could have gone anywhere," says Mum, coming after me. "Bloody school holidays. Six weeks and they don't know what to do with themselves." She catches me up. "What time was this?"

"Half past two," a voice butts in. It's Mickey Finch from next door. He is looking over the fence that separates us.

"Did you see'em?" says Mum.

"I'd just come out for a fag," says Mickey. He's fifteen and just left school. He shouldn't smoke, but he nicks his Dad's Woodbines, and thinks he's smart because his Dad hasn't found out yet. He let me puff on one once. It made me feel sick.

"They came through our garden," Mickey says, "Real sneaky, 'cos they didn't want to be seen. They had cakes."

"Cakes!" my Mum splutters, "Where'd they get cakes?"

Mickey seemed to know everything. "I think Jenny Mynard got them from her house. Bottles o' pop an' all."

Mum is flabbergasted. Then she remembers what she really wants to know. "Where'd they go?"

"Ah, well," Mickey says, realising he might have said too much. "I'm sorry, I never meant no harm.

"Mickey, what have you done?"

Mickey pulls his face all shapes, trying to make up his mind. At last, he decides to own up. "They wanted to know where they could go." He stops, gulps, and then goes on again. "For an adventure." Gulp. "So I said, did they know where." gulp, " the Red Barn was? They seemed dead keen when I told them about the murder."

"You told'em how to get there?" says Mum, "The Red Barn?"

And I say, "What murder?"

"Don't you know?" says Mickey, and he seems to enjoy the story." Tracey Lomax. They found her in the Red Barn. She'd been strangled. He grinned at a juicy bit. "She had no knickers on."

"That's enough o' that," my Mum says. "You'd no business sending two young girls up there."

The long row of houses where we live, backs on to fields. Most of the fences have home-made gates put into them. Kids go through to play football or cricket. When I've made my balsa wood glider I shall fly it there.

"Right, Mickey Finch," says Mum, jabbing him with a finger. "You can go across to Jenny Mynard's and tell her Mum what's happened. We'll go up the fields and see if we can find the girls."

"I want to finish my glider."

"You'll come with me," says Mum, "I don't want to lose both of you." Then she sees Mickey Finch is still standing there. "Are you still here?" she says and jabs him again.

"All right," says Mickey, "Don't poke. I'm going," and he drags himself to the front gate towards the Mynard's house. I see him pull a squashed cake from his pocket and take a bite.

"Bribery and corruption," says Mum, and shouts after him, "And tell Mrs Mynard you're sorry."

She drags me down the garden path, out through the gate, and then we follow a narrow track towards the Red Barn - I suppose. I've never been to the Red Barn, but we don't get that far. A few houses along we see Mrs Langley hanging out some washing, and she calls across to us.

"Are you looking for your Sally?"

"Yes."

"She was with another girl. They went into the playground."

Further on there is a gap between the houses. You can get to it from the road, but there's a way in from the field as well. There's a roundabout, some swings, a seesaw, and a slide.

There doesn't seem to be anyone there, but then we hear voices.

Jenny Mynard's head appears above the rail at the top of the slide. "Do you want some cake?" she calls down.

Sally's head pops up next to her. "We drank all the pop," she says, "We pretended it was champagne 'cos we've climbed Everest."

"We climbed up the slidey side," adds Jenny. "We're having an adventure."

"Well, next time, don't just run off. I've been worried sick. We thought you'd gone to the Red Barn. I didn't want you going up there. Anything could have happened to you."

The girls began to come down, slowly, down the steps, not down the slidey side.

"Sorry, mum" says Sally.

"Sorry," says Jenny Mynard.

"Can we go home?" I say, "The glue'll be set on my glider."

We walk back down the road side, and drop off Jenny Mynard at home. Her Mum tells her off for helping herself to the cakes without asking, and for running off without telling anybody. "Don't you ever do that again," she says.

My mum says, "Did you give Mickey Finch what for?"

"I did," says Mrs Mynard, "And do you know what he said?"

"What?"

"Had I any more cake? It was delicious."

"He'll go far, that one," says my Mum, "If he doesn't end up in jail."

When we get home, we have tea, and Sally has to go to bed early with another sharp word from Mum about going off without saying where she's going. Then she tucks her in and gives her a kiss.

"Perhaps your brother'll read you a story," she says.

"Famous Five," Famous Five," says Sally.

I take a book off the shelf.

"Which one is it?" asks Sally.

I chuckle. "Famous Five Go Adventuring Again," I tell her, but don't go getting ideas.

Sisters! I read two pages, and she is asleep.

Mouse Meeting

Mick said he was Mortified.

Idris said he was Indignant.

Colin said he was Catatonic even though he hated cats and would not have regarded any member of the feline species as a tonic.

Eric said he was emasculated, even though he didn't know what it meant but was eager to be initially designated with the other three mice.

The four mice had once chewed their way through four-hundred-pages of a dictionary acquiring as they did so, a broad vocabulary but very little learning.

In short, they were angry.

"We have been misused," said Mick.

"Intimidated," said Idris in the musical squeaks of a Welsh mouse. He had arrived at the house as a stowaway in a package of Caerphilly cheese, of which there had been little left when it was unwrapped by the recipient. Idris had jumped out and scuttled downstairs to the basement where the other three received him warmly.

"We have been clobbered," said Colin.

"Extirpated," said Eric.

"I shall call an extraordinary meeting of the Ministry of Independence, Co-operation and Equality (MICE)," said Mick. At the back of the dictionary there had been an Appendix consisting of a list of acronyms and abbreviations which Mick had found so fascinating he had taken to inventing his own. The people upstairs, for instance, were referred to as PUS.

The People Upstairs (PUS) were in fact a mother and her two daughters - three frightful excrescences of humanity left over from a fairytale in which they had subjected their stepdaughter/stepsister Ella to the most dreadful cruelties and humiliation. They had forced her to live in the basement, only emerging to wait upon them when it was time for food to be served, fires to be re-fuelled, beds to be made or cleaning duties to be carried out. Ella had become an unhappy drudge whose only friends were the mice.

"But she has abandoned us," said Idris with, surprisingly for a mouse, the thunderous roar, of a storm brewing amongst the Welsh hills.

"Meeting at midnight," said Mick, and the others noted the significance of the hour.

On the landing that led to the top of the stairs leading down to the basement, stood a grandfather clock keeping time and providing occasional amusement for the four mice who delighted acting out the popular rhyme "Hickory Dickory Dock" by taking it in turns to run up or down according to the hour. As they were only supposed to run down on the stroke of one, they would cheat by hitting the dome of the chime with a toffee hammer which Idris had discovered in the pantry when searching for tit bits.

The clock was working its sonorous way up to twelve midnight as the mice assembled for their meeting. By the time it struck the twelfth chime, they were seated on toy building blocks around a large cotton reel which served as a table. Mick stood up on his back paws, straightened his whiskers and assumed the role of chairman.

"Gentlemice," he began, "We are meeting to consider a plan of action in the light of our recent humiliation, but first we must honestly admit that the humiliation followed a time of glorious excitement, transfiguration, elation, and elevation.

The others heard him with rapt attention. Mick had been first to discover the dictionary in a basement cupboard and had eaten a great many pages before the others had joined him at the feast. He was therefore possessed of an eloquence they much admired, even if they didn't always understand what he was saying.

"Hear, hear," said Colin.

"Thank you, my honourable mouse-mate," said Mick.

"Is this about Ella?" asked Eric. "I liked Ella."

"We all liked her," said Mick, "but the fact remains that once she had gone up to the palace with Prince Charming and married him, she didn't want to know us anymore."

"Hear, hear," said Colin.

"After all we'd done," said Idris, "conducting the resistance movement against those three harridans upstairs: chewing holes in their stockings, depositing droppings in their underwear drawers. Irritants they were, and irritants is what they got."

"I liked the jingly bits on the harness," said Eric. "That was fun. I liked being a pony, pulling the pumpkin coach."

"By heck, didn't we gallop hell for leather when it were close on midnight," said Idris.

"Hear, hear," said Colin.

"All the same," Mick insisted, "After all the glory of the occasion, we were left high and dry, forgotten, as though our support for Ella was a thing of no importance to her."

"Hear, hear," said Colin.

"I made friends with a frog," said Eric. "Didn't they look smart in their footmen's outfits; I wouldn't have minded being a footman."

"Hear, hear," said Colin.

"Honourable mouse-mate Colin," said Mick, puffing himself up, "Do we have your full attention?"

"Hear, hear," said Colin.

"Ignore him," said Idris, "I think he's been at the Gorgonzola. Do you have a plan, honourable mouse-mate Mick?"

"It is the particular purpose of this parliament to perorate and properly propose a potential plan," answered Mick.

"Did you eat all the P's?" asked Colin, suddenly awake.

"Possibly and probably," said Idris with a guffaw, "but I ate those."

"I'm tired," said Eric, "I'm going to bed," and he left the table.

Mick, despite his prolific mastery of the P section of the dictionary had run out of patience. Perseverance patently eluded him. "Meeting postponed," he announced," and smiled when he realised that *postponed* gave him two P's for the price of one.

The meeting was never to be recalled. Later that morning, a messenger arrived from the Palace. He carried an envelope addressed to the Mice, but which was at first intercepted by the People Upstairs (PUS). To offset their disappointment that the envelope with its royal crest was not for them, they clumped down the basement steps behind him.

With much excited squeaking, the Mice scrambled to stand in front of the messenger who, much to Eric's delight was the same frog who had served as a footman on the grand occasion of the Royal Ball.

The Messenger smiled, and out of pleased recognition and sheer favouritism handed the envelope to Eric. Mick was inevitably a bit miffed, but took no offence when he saw that the envelope was large enough to contain four smaller envelopes, each addressed personally to Mick, Idris, Colin, and Eric (MICE).

Each envelope had in it an invitation to a ceremony to be held at the Palace this coming Saturday. Each of the Mice were to be awarded with an MBE (Mouse's Best Endeavours), and further invited to make a new home for themselves at the Palace.

The People Upstairs (PUS) immediately ranted, raved, and ran back up to take to their beds and weep copiously at the unfairness of it all.

The four mice, danced with glee in the knowledge that Ella had not forgotten them after all. (TALHEA).

Christmas Cottage

"That's nice," Evie said.

"Not very Christmassy," said Graham.

They were sitting side by side on the sofa, sifting through the latest pile of Christmas cards to have slid through the letter box. Out of its envelope Evie had pulled a card depicting a wildflower meadow with cypress trees in the middle distance framing a white-washed cottage with open dormer windows. A cloudless blue sky topped a flawless summer scene. Not a photograph, a reproduction of an oil painting, and as Graham had observed, not very Christmassy.

"It's probably the south of France or somewhere." he went on. "Do they have Christmas in France?"

"Ooh, you are daft," said Evie. "Could you live there?"

"Don't speak French."

"You could learn."

"I've given up learning for Christmas."

"No," said Evie, "That's Lent."

"What is?"

"What you give things up for. That's *Lent*."

"Who to? Who's borrowed it, and when are we going to get it back?"

Evie gave up. Graham was in one of his moods, when he wouldn't take anything seriously. She put it down to the approach of Christmas, and the imminent descent of their respective families. He would have to be on his best behaviour.

She waved the unseasonal Christmas card under his nose.

"We could be happy somewhere like this. It's idyllic."

"Do you mean idiotic?"

"Oh, Graham. Be romantic for a minute. It'd be peaceful. Away from it all."

"Mmm," pondered Graham, "I bet it's a long way from the Co-op."

"You wouldn't need the Co-op. There'd be a farm shop, with homemade butter, croissants, baguettes, fresh meat, milk, cheese…." Evie's eyes began to glaze over at the prospect of rural tranquility and warm, continental sunshine.

Graham brought her down to earth. "Do you think it would have a shed?" I bet its miles from a B&Q." Then, the crunch question, "You're not serious, are you?"

"I was just dreaming, that's all. That's the trouble with you men. You don't dream. You've no ambition."

"I've always had ambition," said Graham, his voice and demeanour suddenly tinged with regret.

"What about?"

"This house," he said glumly, looking round at the immaculate lounge and beyond, through a cleanly sculpted archway to an equally immaculate dining area. Pristine white walls and carefully placed pots of flowers and plants, well-chosen ornaments, and pictures – mostly Evie's contribution – completed the look of a house which even after ten years had failed to acquire any character. Graham had decided the house simply didn't have the potential.

They had gone for new build when the bank had moved Graham to Bath. The bank had been generous with the removal allowance. They had wanted him there in a hurry. It hadn't given Graham and Evie much time to look round. The house was on a bland new estate, mostly semis with a hint of Athens and little space between them. The estate agent had advertised it as 'Architect designed. Ready to move into. Superb professional finish.' Graham had been glad of that at first. While they were both still working and Graham was trying to establish himself in a new post, he didn't want the bother of redecorating, changing into overalls after tea and climbing ladders with paint and brushes, so he hadn't troubled himself, and been content with episodes of Lewis and Endeavour. As a house, it was clean, convenient, and comfortable, but it wasn't really home. It certainly wasn't *his*. He had known it was a mistake from the first Sunday morning, when he looked down the road to see half a dozen or so middle-aged men on their front drives, washing their Volvos. Evie had done her best but only tinkered at the edges without much enthusiasm. He guessed it wasn't really her home either, just somewhere they ate and slept and were now living together in early retirement. Was that why she was hinting at moving to a cottage in the country?

Graham jumped up. He surprised himself as well as Evie. "Let's bloody do it," he said, grabbing the card from her and waving it about. "Let's find a cottage in the country, somewhere that needs a bit of TLC. Something we can put our own stamp on, really make it ours. Some soulless couple will jump at this – this pale, perfect Parthenonic clinic – Can you say Parthenonic? – Anyway, you know what I mean. It was a mistake for us, but somebody will pay a pretty city price for it, and we can use the proceeds to buy a ramshackle property in need of love and restoration. And we'll make it ours."

Evie stood up now, and put her arms around him, crumpling the Christmas card between them. "Oh, Graham! How long have you been storing this up? Has it been so disappointing?"

There was a pool of silence into which Graham slowly sank after years of treading water. Then he surfaced.

"The thing is, "Graham said, leading her back to the sofa and sitting her down again, sitting next to her. "The thing is – when the bank offers you promotion and says, 'How'd you like to go to Bath?' it seems like the chance of a lifetime; recognition for all my hard work, and the prospect of living in this elegant city. I mean, there was nothing wrong with Huddersfield, but Bath seemed a step up. The bank knew it and they wanted a quick decision to replace my predecessor. It was all such a rush. When you feel flattered and valued and you don't want to seem ungrateful, least of all unco-operative, well…"

"Well?"

"You tend to lose your sense of perspective…..." Graham sighed and fizzled out for a moment, and then, tentatively, began again. "I did. I lost my way and took you with me. I'm sorry."

"Don't be. It's what wives do."

"What?"

"Stand by their man." she said with a Dolly Parton drawl. She grinned. Her eyes twinkled.

Graham put down the Christmas card and took her hands in his. "I love you, Evie Smith."

Evie picked up the card and smoothed it on her lap. "Shall we do it, then?" she said.

"Do you mean it?" Graham said, "Really? Go back to Huddersfield?"

"Somewhere up there. Well, no, *anywhere*, it doesn't matter; wherever we can find a tumbledown cottage at a knockdown price; money left over for the renovations, and the challenge of making a home out of a ruin. She held the card up to his face. "And if it hasn't got a shed, we'll get one."

"You're on," said Graham, and kissed her. It was going to be a happy new year.

Tonsorial Artist

"Why does it say tonsilitis?"

David was eight and quite proud of being able to say *tonsilitis*.

He was standing with Norman, his father, on the pavement outside the hairdressers in Cook Street.

"Where does it say *tonsilitis*?" his father said.

"Up there," David pointed. A sign hung above the hairdressers. It read: *Derek Thomas, Tonsorial Artist*.

"No," said Norman, "not *tonsilitis, tonsorial.*"

"Ton - sor – ial," David said, stretching his face to get his tongue round it, "Is that like a tyrannosaurus?"

"No," said Norman, "It's to do with having your hair done. A posh name for a barber."

"Oh," said David, "Is Derek posh?"

Norman couldn't resist what he thought was a sublime piece of wit. "I suppose he thinks he's a cut above the rest," he chuckled. He looked at David. "Cut? Above the rest?" It was too sublime for an eight-year-old.

Norman had been coming to the tonsorial artist in Cook Street for years. When David was ready for a haircut, he had brought him too. Derek called David, David, and didn't mind David calling him Derek. If David sat still while Derek was cutting his hair, Derek would reward him with a lollipop or let him choose from a jar of liquorice allsorts.

As they waited for the barbers to open, Tom Jenkins came round the corner and joined them. "Is he not open, yet?" said Tom, "It's nearly nine." He rattled the door handle to no avail.

"We were here at quarter to," said Norman, "No sign of Derek." The 'Sorry, We're Closed' sign still hung behind the glass door.

Norman and Tom fell into conversation. They were workmates at Parbold's Bakery and would meet again when the afternoon shift clocked on at three, but still had plenty to chat about. David felt invisible.

"I'm going to see Mr Wag," he said suddenly.

"What for?" asked Norman.

"I have to get a notebook for school," and David ran off to the corner shop. It was a regular calling point for children on their way to school, mostly for sweets or comics. Mr Waghmare was always pleased to see them.

The shop bell tinkled as David entered the Aladdin's cave of groceries, tinned goods, cereals, stationery, sweets, and newspapers.

"Good morning, Master David," said Mr Waghmare, "Sweets, is it? You will spoil your teeth."

"Good morning, Mr Wag, I have to buy a notebook."

"Writing, then. What are you going to write?"

"Mr Forshaw wants us to write a diary while we are on half term. Fifty words a day. It's not fair, it's supposed to be a holiday."

"It will be a good discipline for you," said Mr Waghmare. "What will you write about today?"

"I don't know," said David, "Nothing special happens."

"Back in India," said Mr Waghmare, "I have an uncle. He is an old man now, but he is a writer. I will tell you what he told me once: *A writer does not sit about waiting for interesting things to happen so that he can write about them. He writes about ordinary things and makes them interesting.*"

"Ordinary is just ordinary," said David.

"Well," Mr Waghmare went on, "if that doesn't work, then use your imagination. That's another thing my uncle said: *Imagination makes everything work.* Now, is this the sort of notebook you're looking for?" Mr Waghmare had taken a slim exercise book from a shelf. He held it out for David to inspect.

"Did Mr Forshaw not give you a book for your homework?"

"I can't find it," David confessed, "I think I dropped it on the way home. Mr Forshaw will be cross."

"Not if you write him something really interesting in you new book. He will be pleased that you've replaced the book so that you can do your homework."

"You don't know Mr Forshaw," said David, taking the exercise book. It had a glossy silver cover that reflected the shop lights and threw flickering shapes over the shelves. "It's a bit posh for a diary. How much is it?"

"I tell you what," said Mr Waghmare, "We'll do a deal. If you promise to come back at the end of the week and show me what you have written, I will give you the book for free."

David's eyes glistened. "Wow! Thank you, Mr Wag."

The shop bell tinkled, and David's father came in.

"Is he being a nuisance Mr Wag?"

"Not at all, not at all. We are about to close a deal. Promise David?"

"Promise, Mr Wag."

"What are you promising, David?"

"Mr Wag is giving me this book for free, if I show him my writing."

"I see," said Norman, though he didn't. Surely, even nice respectable Indians like Mr Waghmare wouldn't give something away for nothing. Norman had no reason to be suspicious, but he was.

"Anything I can get for you?" Mr Waghmare enquired.

"Not unless you can do us a couple of short back and sides," said Norman.

"Ah, yes, Barber Derek is shut today. He came in very early for his paper and told me his mother had been taken ill, and he would be going to see her."

"Where did he go?" asked David.

"None of your business," his father said briskly, and then turned back to Mr Waghmare. "Where *did* he go?"

"Manchester, I expect. It's where his mother lives. He said she's in hospital. He took the train. It's a long way Manchester."

"Is he coming back?" asked David.

"All depends, I suppose."

"Does it?

"On what's wrong with her. How long she's in for."

"You never know what's just around the corner, do you? Come on, David, we'd better be going."

They said goodbye to Mr Waghmare, David tucked his new notebook into his pocket, and the shop bell tinkled as they shut the door behind them.

....

Half Term Diary

By David Porter

<u>Monday</u>

Me and my dad went to the Tonsorial Artists in Cork Street to have our hair cut. He opens at half past eight and we were there at quarter to nine, but he was shut. We waited a bit, and dad's mate from work came. He tryd the door but there was nobody there. A Tonsorial artist is not like a tyrannosaurus or any other sort of dinosaur. He just cuts hair and looks like a human bean. My dad says he doesn't cut hair any longer. Cos it has to be cut shorter, which he larfs at cos he thinks it's a sort of joke. I don't. I went into Mr Wag's shop to get a notebook and Mr Wag gave me one for free slongas I show him this riting. Mr Wag is Indian but he talks just like eveyboddy else. He told us Tonsorial Derek had gone to Manchester becos his Muther had tonsilitis.

<u>Tuesday</u>

Dad phoned the Tonsorial Artist , but there was no anser, so we have not had our hairs cut . I stayed in and watched some rubbish quiz show on telly cos my mum likes it. She does the irning while she watches and whoops when somebody wins. I watched the first bit of a horror film when Mum went out to the kitchin for a cup of joos. When she saw the knifes and the blood she made me switch it off. I can't think of anything else to rite today.

<u>*Wednesday*</u>

I thnk Mr Wag is going to be dispointde wth me if I show him this cos nothig good is happnin. My imagination – I lookd that up so as to spel it rite - can't think of anything eether. Everthng is ordinary.

<u>*Thursday*</u>

Derek the Tonsorial Artist came back from Manchester. I think Manchester does weerd things to people. Derek has now got long hair and teeth like sizzers. They go snip snappity snip when he chews a lickrish all sort. He keeps lickerish all sorts in a jar an he gives them to little boys who don't wriggle in the barbers chair. If they wriggl he pokes them with the sizzers until they bleed. The blood drips on the flor and it makes the hair that's on the floor get sticky so that it sticks to your shoes when you go out, and you make red footprints on the pavement all the way home. My mum yelled at me because shed just mopped the kitchen floor. My dad dint make a mess on the floor cos he took his shoes off at the door, but he stepped where I'd bin, and he got blood on his soks.

Friday

We went to the Tonsorial Artist toady and he was open, so me and my dad both had our hair cut. My dad had an itch so he wriggled in the chair to scratch it. The Tonsorial Artist was mad at him and stabbed him with the sizzers and told him to sit still or he'd fetch the hedge clipers. So my dad sat still after that and Derek gave him a lollipop. It was a lemon lolly and my dad said it was too sharp, so he give it to me and I dint mind it bein sharp so I ate it all. I even swallowed th stick to show that I am a fierce warror who can tacle anything. Wen I am bigger I will be a Tonsorial monster and I will chew anything to bits with teeth like shovels and I will terrerize the neighborhood and the workers in the bakery until they all dies of tonsilitis and nothing will be oridnry anymore. Amen.

....

Mr Forshaw collected in the children's diaries and took them home to read. He liked to develop their creativity, and write some encouraging comment at the end, but when he read David Porter's contribution, for once in his life he had no idea what to say.

He knew that however much writers thought their stories were pure fiction, there was always something lurking in the roots of them that had begun in living experience.

When he read David's diary for a second time, he wondered what that experience might be, but he couldn't bring himself to read it again.

Mystery Man

"Do you fancy going down to the river," said Colin.

Fiona didn't need much inviting. It was a warm summer night with a full moon. "Are you asking me out?" she said, "Is this a date?"

"If you like," said Colin. Fiona did like. She had seen Colin from a distance in the Sixth Form Centre at Burntwood High School. She'd watched him fooling about with the other lads, but not so as to make himself look silly. He had restraint and knew when to stop. Nonetheless he had not been afraid to ask her to go to the river with him.

Colin had not expected to be dismissed out of hand. He had a feeling that blonde, smiley Fiona would be amenable. It didn't need a lot of courage to ask her.

"I've got chocolate," he said, "Do you want some?"

"Down by the river, "said Fiona, "It'll be like a picnic. Have you got any money?"

"Skint," said Colin, "only had enough for the chocolate."

"My treat then," said Fiona, "we can call in at the off licence and get some drinks."

"You're all right, you are," Colin said, "Let's go." He took her hand, and she didn't resist, so they walked together down Miller Street towards the Embankment.

At the corner of Cook Street, they went into Mr Ghani's Convenience Store and Fiona bought a couple of milk shakes. Then they went through the Embankment gates and down the sloping path amongst the trees and shrubs until they reached a long bench at the river's edge. On the grass behind them plump bundles snickered and shifted and turned out to be ducks sleeping in shadowy hollows.

Colin and Fiona sat down, not too close but friendly. There were lamps along the embankment that lit the underside of the trees and made quivering reflections in the water.

"Fairyland," said Fiona. "Have you been down here a lot?"

Colin broke the bar of chocolate open and offered her a piece. She took it and said, "Ooh, Galaxy. Posh chocolate."

"I've been down here before," said Colin, "Susie Fletcher said it was a nice place." He hesitated, wondering whether he really wanted to share this with Fiona on a first date.

"Fairyland," repeated Fiona, "All lights and magical reflections."

"Not with Susie Fletcher it wasn't. She tried to get me into the bushes for a full-on snog. Hands all over."

"Oh Colin! Do you really want me to know this?

"Well, if I don't tell you, Susie Fletcher will. You and me could be good friends, but Susie Fletcher might open her big mouth and try to spoil it, just to get her own back. She'll say I jilted her or something and it was all my fault. Do you know, she was stinky."

"Stinky?"

"Like a chip shop. No. egg and bacon. Weird."

Fiona was quiet for a bit. "Here," she said at last, "drink your milk shake." She handed him the bottle. Then she said, "Susie Fletcher thinks she's a hot property. Boys who fall for her are likely to get their fingers burned."

"Not just their fingers," added Colin. Fiona gave him a surprised look.

"Oops. Sorry," Colin said, "Gone too far." Then Fiona sniggered. Colin joined in and then they were both laughing and spilling their milk shakes. It was as though they had known each other forever.

They chatted, drank their milkshakes and finished the chocolate. There was a waste bin further along the embankment. Colin offered to take the empty bottles and chocolate wrapper and dispose of them.

"I'll just sit here," said Fiona, "Then you'd better see me home."

"Great," said Colin, "Shan't be a tick."

He was more than a tick. He was several minutes. The bin was crammed full so that the milkshake bottles rolled back out through the slot, and he had to chase after them to prevent them rolling into the river. He pushed an arm in through the slot and squashed the contents down, so they were well in. The bottles stayed put then and he made his way back to Fiona, stopping suddenly before he reached her, because she appeared to be in deep conversation with a tall man in a flat cap who, as Colin watched, sat down next to her.

"Hey!" Colin shouted. The man stood up and walked away at a good speed. Colin went quickly to Fiona and put an arm round her. "You all right?"

"Yeah, he didn't touch me or anything. He just talked."

"What about?"

"He said he had a daughter like me."

"What did that mean? Like you?"

"Search me," said Fiona, "He said he didn't see her anymore, 'cos his wife had cleared off and taken the daughter with her. He said he missed her."

"Lonely rejected old man," said Colin, "Sounds as though I came back just in time. He'd have had you for his daughter and who knows what else. I wonder why they left him."

"I think we should go." Fiona said. She stood up. Colin took her hand.

Suddenly, flashing blue lights bounced off the trees and the water as a police car drove through the Embankment gateway. A siren blared, disturbing the ducks and generating a cacophony of panicked flapping and quacking. There was a slamming of doors and the clump of unhurried footsteps.

"Do you think they're after mystery man?" said Colin.

Before Fiona could answer, an officious voice called out to them. "Are you supposed to be down here at this time of night?"

Colin responded. "I have to be home by half past ten.

"And the girl?"

"The same," answered Fiona, "We were just going."

"You'll talk to us first," the police officer said. His colleague took out a notebook, asked for their names and addresses and wrote them down.

"Have you seen a tall man in a raincoat and flat cap?" said the first.

"Yes," said Fiona.

"Did he talk to you?"

"Yes, but he cleared off when he saw Colin."

"He went that way," said Colin, pointing,

"Did he smell funny?" the policeman with the notebook wanted to know, "Like he'd been in a kitchen cooking fried food?"

"Chip fat." Colin said to himself, but the officer heard him.

"Possibly. Sounds as though it might be our man. You got mobiles?"

"Yes."

"See him again, ring this number." He handed each of them a card." We might catch him at the other end of the path. Thanks for your help,

The police left them, turned the car and drove away. The ducks settled down.

"I want to go home," said Fiona, "Sorry. It was nice."

"Don't be sorry. It was good till the mystery man arrived. Where do you live?"

Fiona told him, so he walked her home, and she kissed him on the cheek when they parted. "Funny first date," she thought.

Colin thought the same.

When they met in the Sixth Form Common Room next day, Fiona had a copy of that morning's Nottingham Post. They sat together and read with increasing horror.

DOUBLE MURDER IN WEST BRIDGFORD

After a police chase through the city last night, a Wilford man was arrested and charged with murder. Gerald Fletcher. 47 was apprehended on the river path near West Bridgford and charged with murdering his estranged wife Gloria 42, and their daughter Susie, 17, at their apartment in Millicent Road.

It is understood from neighbours that Mr Fletcher, whose wife and daughter had left him six months ago because "he had become impossible to live with" was planning yesterday to attempt a reconciliation with the aid of a "glorious fry-up" which was a popular meal in the family when they were together. Bert Freeman, 52, a friend of Mr Fletcher and a local butcher told the Nottingham Post that he had supplied Mr Fletcher with sausages, bacon, eggs and other groceries yesterday afternoon. Mr Fletcher apparently arrived at his wife's apartment about

5.00 p.m., broke in and started to prepare the fried meal for the three of them to sit down and eat on his wife's and daughter's return from work and school when they would discuss things and come to some agreement about their future together. In the event, it was reported by neighbours that "an almighty row" had broken out and Mr Fletcher was seen departing the house in a hurry about 5.30 p.m. Mary Simmons, 64, who had befriended Mrs Fletcher and her daughter when they first moved in, went to check on them and discovered their bodies sprawled on the kitchen floor. "There was a stink of fried food and blood everywhere," said Mrs Simmons, "I called the police at once and told them I had seen Mr Fletcher heading towards the city. I've not seen a murder before. I was quite upset. You don't expect things like that to happen in West Bridgford."

There were sightings of Mr Fletcher throughout the evening, including an encounter with him by a teenage couple on the Embankment who were able to point the police in his direction.

Fiona and Colin stopped reading and looked at each other.

"Blimey," said Colin.

"Are we a *couple*?" asked Fiona.

"It says so in the paper," said Colin, "so it must be true."

"Anyway," Fiona said, "our mystery man is not a mystery anymore."

"Yes, and next time I think we'll not go down to the Embankment."

"Next time?" queried Fiona.

"If that's OK," said Colin.

Fiona paused, her face giving nothing away. Colin was on tenterhooks.

"OK," said Fiona, and Colin took her hand and squeezed it. "I'll bring some more chocolate," he said.

"Great," said Fiona, "and I'll get the milkshakes."

"And I'll watch out for a man in a flat cap stinking of chip fat."

"That's not really funny," said Fiona,

"No," said Colin, but they laughed anyway as though they had known each other forever.

Not The Two Ronnies

"Have you signed in before?" the receptionist said.

Harry stood looking blankly at the touch screen in the Medical Centre.

"Whatever happened to pen and paper?" he muttered, and tentatively prodded the screen with an index finger.

The screen changed to display the months of the year and asked him to touch the month of his birth, which he obediently, but reluctantly did. "It'd be easier if I just told you." he said to the receptionist. She wore a white coat with a label on it. "Flame". Whatever kind of name was "Flame"? What could her parents have been thinking? If she was a horse, she might have been called "Flame"and not raised any eyebrows, but she was blonde, pretty, and Harry thought if he was forty years younger he would have asked her if she fancied going to the pictures.

"Would you like me to help you?" said Flame, "You put the date in now. I can see you put September. What date in September?"

The screen had changed again, and Harry was confronted with the numerals one to thirty. He smiled at Flame. "I'll not be beaten." He poked at 24, but nothing happened. Flame saw that nothing had happened. "Try pressing the number at the bottom." she said, "It's new, it can sometimes be a bit temperamental."

Harry breathed in deeply, breathed out again, coughed, and suppressed the urge to wrench the machine off the wall and throw it across the waiting room.

"Take a seat," said Flame. "It's Mr Robinson isn't it. I'll get you signed in. The doctor won't be long." She made a few clicks on her keyboard, which was in any case, connected to the screen on the wall, and efficiently signed Harry in.

Harry sat down. He didn't belong in this modern age. Give him the hardware shop, where if all you wanted was a single two-inch number ten screw, you could buy just the one, and not have to buy a packet of ten and not have any use for the other nine.

He was contemplating how things had changed since his days in Dexter's Ironmongers, when the automatic doors swung open and, by some strange coincidence, his old mate Gordon Smith came in and saw Harry sitting all alone, looking glum.

"Well!" said Gordon. "Well! If it isn't my old mate, Harry Robinson. Good to see you. Good to see you. How long has it been?" He sat down next to Harry and gave him a hearty shove, which set off a bout of coughing so fierce that it prompted Flame to emerge from behind her glass screen and tend to Harry with a glass of water and a box of tissues.

"You need to tell the doctor about that," said Flame.

"That's why I'm here," said Harry with a splutter.

"Of course. You all right now?"

Harry nodded. Flame turned briefly to Gordon. "Doctor's running a bit late," she said, "Won't be long."

Harry nodded, and Flame went back to Reception. Gordon watched her as she went, shiny blonde hair flouncing on her shoulders, slim legs teetering on glossy black high heels. Harry saw him eyeing her up.

"Too late," said Harry, "I've already asked her. We're going to the pictures later."

"You're joking!"

"Yeah, I'm joking. Wouldn't give me the time of day, would she? What are *you* doing here?"

Gordon made himself more comfortable. "I've got this leg," he said, grimacing as though in fearful pain.

"Just the one?" said Harry, "I brought both o' mine."

Gordon sniggered but didn't really laugh. Working by his side for over thirty years in Dexter's, he had become used to Harry's quirky sense of humour.

"See anything of Bernard these days," Harry asked.

"Bossy Bernard? No, not for a year or two. When we retired, I always imagined meeting Bernard in the street, and seeing him cross the road, coming up to me to tell me to do up the buttons on my raincoat."

They both laughed at the recollection of Dexter's finicky shop manager.

"Mind you," Harry said, "he was efficient. Never anything out of place. When we did a stocktake, there was never a screw missing. I couldn't say I liked him, but he ran a tight ship."

" I met his wife the other day," Gordon said.

"What? Messy Margaret?"

"In Morrison's. I didn't recognise her at first, but she saw me and came over; asked how I was, and did I find retirement suited me. We had a chat. I asked how Bernard was, and she looked me in the eye and said, "You know, just the same.""

Harry said," I could never understand how they stayed together. He was always so smart and dapper, and she looked as though she'd got dressed in a force eight gale."

"You can see why I never got married," Gordon said. "The prospect of ending up with somebody like Messy Margaret, that's what put me off. Anyway, I got used to being a free agent. You can come and go as you please."

There was a sudden beep then, and a digital sign flashed up a message, "Harry Robinson for Dr. Wong."

Harry stood up and shook hands with Gordon. "Well, it's been good to see you, Gordon, remembering the good old days. We must do it again; meet up in the King's Arms or somewhere. I've still got your phone number."

"Yes, why not? Let's do that," Gordon said. "Now, off you go. Get that cough sorted."

....

When Harry came out of the consulting room with a prescription in his hand, Gordon was still sitting in the waiting room.

"You still here?" said Harry.

Gordon stood up as Flame came out from behind the reception area, pulling on a bright yellow coat. "You and me, we've kept Gordon waiting" she said to Harry. "He only came to meet me out. He's taking me for a Pizza and then we're going to Showcase to see the new James Bond."

Harry sat down. His face wasn't agile enough to register the shock. He watched the automatic doors swing open as Gordon and Flame, arm in arm, made a grand exit. He felt his cough coming on worse than before, and hoped he could get to the Pharmacy before it closed.

Mrs Grace's Journal

Georgina met James when they collided in a corridor at the offices of Goose and Smeathers, Solicitors. James wasn't looking where he was going, having turned to shoot a parting remark to his father who was just disappearing through the double doors behind him. He therefore backed into Georgina sending her pile of books and papers flying, which is how they both ended up on their knees scrabbling to retrieve them.

"I'm so sorry," James said, and as, for a moment, they met face to face, lips almost touching, he concluded, in what he knew was a daft, cliched "love at first sight" sort of way, that his life would be incomplete without her.

"Marry me," he said.

Georgina sat suddenly upright; legs crossed like a small girl sitting on the primary school floor in morning assembly. She watched James as he gathered the last few papers and brought them to her on his knees.

Nearby a door opened and Mrs. Grace, a solemn looking secretary in her fifties, looked out and peered down at them over her glasses. "Did I hear a clatter?"

Georgina got to her feet. "We had a small collision, " she said, "but I think we're all right now."She patted the books . "All in order."

Mrs Grace looked directly at Georgina and widened her eyes. Then, looking quizzically at James, she went back in and closed her door.

Georgina giggled. "Do you think she'll write a report?" she asked.

"I expect so, "said James, "She does that sort of thing."

"Are you going to stay down there, Mr Smeathers? Or are you still in proposal mode?"

"Oh," thought James, "She musn't call me Mr Smeathers. She must call me James, or even Jimmy, wrapping me round with that soft, deep voice. So sensual, yet gentle."

"What?" he finally said.

"Proposal mode," said Georgina, "You asked me to marry you."

James got to his feet, brushing dust from his trouser knees, "Yes, I believe I did." He made a feeble attempt to pull himself together. "You're new."

"Not entirely," said Georgina, "I'm twenty five."

"Oh, not only good looking but witty," thought James. She was irresistible. "Of course," he said, "No, I mean, new to the firm."

"Well, yes, and no. I'm temporary. Here today, gone tomorrow."

"Tomorrow?"

"Well, until the end of the week, while Sandra's in court."

"Ah, Sandra, yes, I see. He didn't see at all really. "How dreams begotten unexpectedly soon fade and die."

"Pardon?"

James didn't realise he'd spoken his thoughts aloud. "Well," he said at last, "if we're not to be married, perhaps you'll let me take you out for dinner."

Georgina hesitated. She glanced back at Mrs Grace's office door. "Your father will be wanting these papers,"" she said. "I'll ring you later when I've checked my diary. OK?"

Mrs Grace's door clicked, but she didn't re-emerge. Georgina left the corridor and James watched her go, and stood, still dreaming, as the double doors rattled together. He had invited her for dinner. She handn't said yes, but she hadn't said no. Where was he going before he collided with her? He couldn't remember, so he went out of the office building altogether to breathe some fresh air in the park on the opposite side of the road.

Mrs Grace was alone in her tiny office, which was mostly for Reception purposes. It had a hatch, through which she could see and greet clients as they entered through the front door, so she had noticed James Smeathers going out. She had also heard the conversation between James and Georgina before they had parted.

It was now twelve twenty-five and near enough lunchtime, Mrs Grace decided for her to take a short break and eat what she referred to as her little "snackeroo". It consisted of a hard-boiled egg, a chunk of cheddar cheese, a stick of celery, and two buttered Ryvita biscuits. In her desk drawer she had, earlier in the week, secreted a bottle of Shiraz. With these simple refreshments she felt equipped to have half an hour or so to herself, and while she was eating and drinking, to bring her journal up to date.

She took her journal, a black leather bound volume, out of her large handbag, opened it at the next clean page and smoothed it with a flat hand. She had long ago decided that the ball point pen was cheap and vulgar. When she began to write it was with the fountain pen which her late husband had given her on her 21st Birthday.

There was a noise on the landing, Cassandra stopped brushing her hair, tightened the cord of her bathrobe, and crossed silently to her bedroom door. On opening it, she was surprised, and yet not really surprised, to see James and Georgina on the landing, on hands and knees, facing each other amidst a tangle of toilet paper which appeared to have unravelled itself from its cardboard tube, and wound itself around them. James wore only boxer shorts, and Georgina appeared to be endeavouring to save her feigned, giggling, naked embarrassment by wrapping herself in paper streamers. They were pastel pink, enhancing her smooth, glistening complexion, Cassandra imagined they were engaging in some inventive kind of foreplay.

Mrs Grace paused to bite on a piece of celery and crunched it thoughtfully. What next? She bit off a piece of mature cheddar and contemplated the power of imagination, and the simplicity of it. She had found it easy to transfer what she had seen in the corridor not half an hour ago, to the spacious landing of a country mansion, and to embroider the action. She would have to change the names, of course. When her novel hit the bookshelves, it wouldn't do at all for friends to say, "Well, Nora, fancy your Georgina getting up to such frolics."

Perhaps she should use a nom-de-plume. Mmm. Perhaps it will never hit the bookshelves. Mmm. What was it James had said in the corridor? "How dreams begotten unexpectedly soon fade and die."

She poured some Shiraz into a tumbler and took a sip, while she looked over what she had written. She envisaged the bodies romping on the soft-carpeted landing and looked down at her own body in its grey cardigan and tweed skirt. She sighed, "Everything is sagging" she thought, limp and listless. Life itself is sagging. Only imagination offers solace and hope." She attempted to put a final full stop to the racy paragraph in her journal but failed. Her fountain pen had run out of ink. Uncharacteristically, she swore, "Oh bugger it."

As she felt the tears welling up, there was a tentative ring of the domed brass bell at the hatch. She stood up and without looking to see who might be waiting for an answer, muttered, "I'm shut."

Then Mrs Grace pressed a button on the internal phone and spoke into the receiver, "I'm sorry Mr Smeathers, I'm not feeling very well, I think I had better go home."

"Of course, if you're ill, you must go. I quite understand, I'll ask Georgina to hold the fort. That'll be fine Mrs Grace. You take care now."

When Goose and Smeathers closed at 5.30 pm., Georgina made a small detour on the way to her own cosy little flat, to call on her mother. She still had her key to the large Edwardian house in which she had grown up, and went in to find that her mother had gone to bed with a hot water bottle. Mrs Grace was sitting propped up against the pillows in a single bed which lay parallel to, but a few feet away from that in which her husband had died of an aneurism, and from which in the early years of their marriage, he had once called across to ask her if she really wanted children. Mrs Grace had once confided to Georgina that when she discovered she was pregnant it had struck her as being little short of immaculate conception.

It had made Georgina giggle. She giggled now. "I know you cried," she said, "when I was sent off to boarding school, and I was really sorry because I thought you would be lonely; but I was glad to be free of Papa's Downton Abbey pretensions; the way he insisted on being called Papa and you Mama. The other girls called him a dry old stick. How did you come to marry him?"

"He asked me," her mother said flatly, " and I said yes." She sighed and then she shrugged. "I was never pretty and vivacious like you, Georgina. I didn't want to be left on the shelf. ' Marry in haste, repent at leisure.' After the wedding my mother took me aside and said,'Nora dear, I'm so glad you've got somebody.' I didn't grieve much when he died, except perhaps for missed opportunities."

"Ah, yes, "said Georgina," That reminds me." She delved into a carrier bag. "You must have been in a rare old state when you left the office. I've brought your snackeroo', what's left of it, and also …" and to her mother's dismay, she held up the journal… "this book of somewhat - what shall I say? – spicy jottings?"

"Oh, yes, I *was* in a tizzy. You've read them?"

"Well, Mr Smeathers put me in Reception and hardly anybody came. Will you publish when it's finished?"

"If I don't run out of steam," her mother said.

"If you can turn an innocent encounter in an office corridor into a steamy liaison on a country house landing, I'd say there was plenty of steam left. You're halfway through this book. I didn't read them all. How many have you written?"

"About fifty. I try to do one a day. It's good therapy."

"You *will* change the names? I see that Nora has become Cassandra. Very sophisticated. What will you call me and Mr Smeathers?"

"I'll have to think about it," her mother said, "Are you going out to dinner with him?"

"No, definitely not. He's what one of the girls at school used to refer to as 'Too wet to hang out.' Besides, he's too young."

"He's nearly forty," her mother said.

Georgina was stunned. "Is he really? He's taking a long time to grow up."

"Yes, I think he's a bit of a disappointment to his father."

"I tell you what, Mama," said Georgina with a grin, "Why don't I let him take me out to dinner. After that I can string him along for a while, and then drop him like a hot potato and watch him weep; and you can write a piece about the fascination of a wicked young woman for a fool of an older man. It would make a perfect Mills and Boon."

"Georgina Grace," said Mrs Grace, "You are a lovely mischievous girl. Where *did* I get you from?"

"From a boring old husband." said Georgina, "Come here."

Mrs Grace flung back the covers, got out of bed, and as she threw her arms around her daughter, she laughed more than she had laughed in a very long time.

As I Walk Out

As I walk out,
She walks in,
Firm physique
Pencil thin.

Business suit,
Sharp and tight,
Leather briefcase,
Black as night.

Face unknown.
I hear, I see,
I know them all,
Detective, me.

Turn around,
Watch her go,
Pace unhurried,
Sure and slow.

Takes the lift,
I take the stairs,
Maybe catch her
Unawares.

At the corner,
Second floor,
Clicking heels,
Opens door.

In she slithers,
Door clicks shut.
Now I know.
Squirming gut.

Quick retreat
Or face the foe?
Neat black letters
C.E.O.

I walk in,
She walks out,
Face contorted,
Lined with doubt.

Pluck up courage.
"Who are you?"

"No one you know,
Where's the loo?

Dead suspicious.
"Follow me."
Take her to
Security.

Search and question,
Nothing learned.
Hot frustration,
Fingers burned.

Who she is,
Never know.
Naught to keep her.
Let her go.

She walks out
Grinning, free.
Questions lurk.
Detective, me.

(The CEO would have praised my vigilance, if only the bomb in the briefcase she had planted under his desk had not blown him to kingdom come, along with my soul, from which every syllable of poetry had, in an instant, been erased).

No rhyme,
No reason,
Tabloid blame,
Silly season.

Take the flack.
Least requirement.
Hasty exit,
Swift retirement.

Life just happens.
Can't rehearse.
Doggerel
From bard to verse.

I walked out.
She walked in.
Not so Grand Finale.
Fin

Printed in Great Britain
by Amazon